this book belongs to

William

children's choice®

ROLAND
THE MINSTREL PIG

by WILLIAM STEIG

Windmill Books and E. P. Dutton · New York

For Maggie

 A Children's Choice® Book Club Edition From Scholastic Book Services

ROLAND THE MINSTREL PIG
Copyright © 1968 by William Steig
Printed in the United States of America. All rights reserved. No part of this
book may be used or reproduced in any manner whatsoever without written
permission except in the case of brief quotations embodied in critical articles
and reviews.

ISBN 0-590-75826-8

There was once a pig named Roland, who played the lute and sang so sweetly that his friends never had enough of listening to him. He was a natural musician—from his hoofs to his snout.

It so happened that he also knew a lot of good jokes and riddles, and could stand balanced on his front legs.

Whenever there was a party, Roland was the first one invited. He could always surprise and delight his friends with new songs—some of which were learned from others, and some of which he composed himself, both words and music.

Dance to your partner—one, two, three—
With merry leaps and gracious bends.
Life is a lark. With spirits free
We'll frisk about till the evening ends.

One day Roland was having tea with two dear friends—
Brian, a donkey, and Wesley, a goose.

"It's a shame," said Wesley, "that your lovely singing
is heard only by the few who know you. In my opinion,
you should be traveling far and wide so that the whole
world might hear and marvel at your voice."

"Yes," agreed Brian the donkey. "You could become
famous and rich. And who, if I may ask, deserves it more?"

Once Roland began thinking along these lines, he could think of nothing else. He dreamed for days of fame and of wealth, and he was no longer satisfied with the life he'd been living.

Finally, on a bright July morning, he said good-bye to all his friends and set out into the world as a wandering minstrel. They were all sorry to see him go, but they felt it was best for him and wished him well. Basil, the elephant, gave Roland a velvet cap with a long plume, and Lorenzo, the dog, gave him a knapsack with a blanket, matches, and other useful things in it.

Roland traveled all day without meeting another living soul.

He grew lonesome, and there were a few times when he wanted to turn back—to go home to his friends.

At night, before saying his prayers and going to sleep,
he sang this sad song:

> Lonely am I as yonder moon
> That roams the empty sky.
> No one's here to hear my tune.
> I'm sad enough to cry.

"Bravo! Bravo!" said a fox, suddenly appearing from behind some trees. "*I* heard your tune. And, I must say, never in my life have I heard such singing! Your voice is as sweet and touching as May violets."

The fox then introduced himself as "Sebastian." Roland introduced himself too, and explained why he was there, all alone and singing.

"Why," said the fox, "I can take you straight to the royal palace to sing before the King himself! He happens to be an old friend of mine."

"That is the highest honor a musician can have," said Roland joyfully. "How lucky I am to have met you!"

"If we walk through the night, we can get there by morning," said Sebastian. "This lovely moon will light our way."

So they started out with brisk steps—Roland dreaming and the fox scheming.

After they had walked a mile or so, the fox asked Roland to regale him with a song. And Roland sang:

Hey, nonny, nonny, this weather is bonny,
The flowers are all in bloom.
Let us be gay as we go on our way
Singing ta-ra, ta-ra-ra, ta-boom.

"It's a shame I'm going to eat him," thought the fox. "It will be a big loss to the world. But eat him I must!"

About midnight they chanced on a tree of early apples. Roland loved apples and ate some that were lying on the ground.

"Have an apple," he said to Sebastian.

"No, thanks," said the fox. "I expect I'll be eating a big meal later on."

Then he slipped away.

Moments later an enormous rock came tumbling down the hill, barely missing Roland. It would have been his end had it hit him.

Sebastian turned up out of nowhere and asked what had happened. Roland told him. (As if the fox didn't know!)

"That's too horrible," said Sebastian. "I can't bear to think about it." But really he had nothing else on his mind.

A little later in their journey, while Roland was resting under a tree, Sebastian again disappeared. Soon a big hornets' nest fell out of the tree, and Roland was beset by hundreds of stinging hornets. Had he not rushed to a nearby pond and thrown himself in, the hornets would have finished him.

Again Sebastian appeared. "Trouble seems to seek you out," he said. "Perhaps a little nap would do us both good. We could resume our journey in the morning, well-rested. Would you sing me a song, please, before we retire?" And Roland sang:

I loved her tail, her ears, her snout,
I loved her form so fair.
She looked at me with glowing eyes;
I walked as if on air.

And they both went to sleep as the moon was setting.

In the morning Roland woke up with a lute string around his neck.
"Now how on earth did that happen?" asked the fox. Roland wondered too.

They walked all morning, and about noon, as Roland was resting on a tree stump, the fox said, "Roland, my friend, I have good news for you. We are not many miles from the King's palace. If you were not a pig, and could climb to the top of that tree, you could see its towers from here. I have an idea. I'll hoist you up!"

So Sebastian got a rope, and soon had Roland hanging in the air.

"I don't see any towers," said Roland, looking around,
"just some fields and a brook."

And then—good heavens—glancing down, he was startled to see Sebastian lighting a fire right under him!

"Just what are you doing?" screamed Roland.

"I'm going to lower you over the fire and roast you," said Sebastian. "What a succulent dish you will make! I think I will add some parsley for seasoning."

Roland realized the fox was not joking, and began to cry. Then he asked for his lute so he could sing one last song. The fox, only too glad to hear Roland sing once more, gave him the lute. Roland, full of emotion, sang more beautifully than he had ever sung before. It was a song he composed that instant:

> *Farewell, dear world, dear hill, dear shore,*
> *Dear butterflies, dear birds, dear bees,*
> *Dear night, dear day, dear seasons four,*
> *Dear flowering fields, dear fruited trees,*
> *Dear warming sun, dear gentle breeze.*
> *My heart's so sore*
> *I'll be no more.*
> *I feel an aching in my knees.*

Meanwhile the King himself, on one of his trips into the countryside, was passing on his palanquin in the woods nearby, and heard Roland's marvelous voice.

Roland dropped his lute and fainted.

"Here, here, what sort of skulduggery is going on in my woods?" roared the King, suddenly confronting Sebastian.

"Just a joke, Your Highness," said the fox, "just a joke."

The King cut the rope with an angry slash of his sword, and Roland fell heavily on Sebastian, knocking him senseless.

"Who are you, strange pig?" asked the King.

"I am Roland," said Roland, "a wandering minstrel. And this fox—Sebastian is his name—promised me a hearing before Your Majesty."

"I heard you," said the King, "just moments ago. And may I say that, though I have heard the world's finest voices, never have I heard one as heavenly as yours. You are supreme!"

Both Roland and Sebastian were taken to the King's palace on the royal palanquin.

There Roland was given a robe of scarlet velvet with a silk lining, and a fine chamber in which to live and study.

Later Roland appeared in court before a distinguished audience of peers
of the realm, who listened in profound
admiration as he sang:

Hail the heavens up above,
Hail to honor, courage, love.
Let these halls with music ring!
All hail His Majesty the King!

Sebastian was put in the dungeon, where he was to live the rest of his years on nothing but stale bread with sour grapes and water.

Roland became world-renowned and wealthy enough to suit any pig's fancy. Along with many other honors, he was awarded the Supreme Medal of Excellence—a golden apple in a cluster of laurel leaves—which, from then on, he always wore around his neck, hanging from a silken band.

The Children's Choice® Clubhouse

It's the perfect place for playing or for curling up with a good book ★ Big enough to hold a few friends (it's 3' x 4½' and 4½' tall) ★ Made of sturdy corrugated cardboard with a washable finish ★ Decorated inside and out with whimsical illustrations in full color ★ A very special gift.

To order, please send your name and address with a check or money order for $19.95 to:

**Children's Choice® Clubhouse
Scholastic Inc.
900 Sylvan Ave.
Englewood Cliffs
New Jersey 07632**